To Flory Jagoda, Keeper of the Flame –DL
To all the brave women of this world –SW

Many thanks to Flory Jagoda for her hospitality (such delicious *börek*!) and hours of conversation; to Susan Gaeta, Flory's musical protégé whose own renditions of Sephardic songs are breathtaking, for introducing me to Flory; and to my friend Karen Simon for introducing me to Susan. I am grateful also to Betty Jagoda Murphy, Flory's daughter, for her helpful review and comments. A final thank-you to ethnomusicologist and performer Judith R. Cohen for her careful review. Any errors are my own responsibility.
–DL

Additional image credits: Wikipedia, pp. 4-7 (map); courtesy of the Jagoda Family, p. 32 (left); Pat Jarrett/Virginia Humanities, p. 32 (right); Alexander Lysenko/Shutterstock.com, p. 32 (key).

Video courtesy of The Virginia Folklife Program, a public program of the Virginia Folklife Program at Virginia Humanities. www.virginiafoundation.org. Flory Jagoda, Susan Gaeta and Howard Bass perform Flory's song "Ocho Kandelikas" at the Richmond Folk Festival on October 14, 2012.

KAR-BEN PUBLISHING, INC.
A division of Lerner Publishing Group, Inc.
241 First Avenue North
Minneapolis, MN 55401 USA
1-800-4-KARBEN

Website address: www.karben.com

Main body text set in Baskerville Com regular 16/20.
Typeface provided by Linotype AG.

Library of Congress Cataloging-in-Publication Data

Names: Levy, Debbie, author. | Wimmer, Sonja, illustrator.
Title: The key from Spain : Flory Jagoda and her music / by Debbie Levy ; illustrated by Sonja Wimmer.
Description: Minneapolis : Kar-Ben Publishing, [2019] | Series: Kar-Ben favorites | Summary: Just as her ancestors were forced to leave Spain during the Inquisition, Flory flees Europe for a new life in the United States, bringing with her a precious harmoniku and a passion for Ladino music.
Identifiers: LCCN 2018032671| ISBN 9781541522183 (lb : alk. paper) | ISBN 9781541522190 (pb : alk. paper)
Subjects: LCSH: Jagoda, Flory—Juvenile fiction. | CYAC: Jagoda, Flory—Fiction. | Refugees—Fiction. | Sephardim—Fiction. | Music—Fiction. | Bosnian Americans—Fiction.
Classification: LCC PZ7.L58258 Ke 2019 | DDC [E]—dc23

LC record available at https://lccn.loc.gov/2018032671

Manufactured in the United States of America
1-44401-34662-10/1/2018

The Key from Spain

FLORY JAGODA and Her Music

by Debbie Levy   illustrated by Sonja Wimmer

KAR-BEN
PUBLISHING

Long ago, in a place called Al-Andalus in the land of Spain,
there was a time of dazzling music and science,
art and poetry, map-making and mathematics,
and harmony among neighbors—
Muslims, Jews, and Christians.

CASTILE
Tomelloso
Almanza
Herrera
Villa havla
Cividad-real
Almagro
Albacete
Chinchilla
Orellana
Abenoya
Almadovar
Val de pernas
Cozar
Allamilla
Duenos
Segare
Tolosa
MURCIA
Andujar
Barza
Adarnuz
Cordova
Velez
Palma
Montilla
Bazu
Finana
Estepa
Osuna
Antequera
Vera
Purchena
Mujacar
Almeria
Adra
St. Lazaro
St. Pedro
Ronda
Muas
Molina
Estepona
MED
Tarfogaret
Melilla

Many years passed.

New rulers conquered the land.
The new king and queen said to the Jews:
"You are not welcome here! *Leave!*"
Jewish families left Spain.
The Altaras family was one of them.

The Altarases journeyed first to Turkey,
   later to Bosnia, always carrying two precious possessions with them.
One was very little: a key.
The other was very big, yet took up no space at all:
Ladino.

Ladino, the language of the *Sephardim*,
   the Jews from Spain.
Ladino, a language made from many languages,
   from Spanish and Hebrew and Arabic.
Ladino, the language the *Sephardim* spoke at home.

"the key from Spain"
La yave de Espanya

1568

"tiya"
aunt

"nona"
grandmother

"nonu"
grandfather

1870

In the tiny mountain village of Vlasenica,
the Altarases again lived in harmony among
their neighbors.
They became a large family, with *Nona* and *Nonu* and *tiyas*
and uncles and cousins,
more than forty members strong, including . . .

a girl named Flory.

She grew up with Jewish, Muslim, and Christian friends, with neighbors of different faiths living and working side by side, like her ancestors before her.

1923

Flory and her family spoke Ladino at home,
    Bosnian in the village.
They sang—and sang and sang and sang!—
    in both languages.

No village celebration was complete
    without The Singing Altaras Family
    making music into the wee hours,
Sephardic and Bosnian melodies,
    voices trilling, hands clapping, guitars,
    mandolins, tamburitzas,
    and tambourines pulsing the rhythms.
Songs filled the sky.
Music filled Flory's heart.

Nona filled Flory's heart, too,
  not only with her songs and guitar-playing
  and kitchen drawer overflowing with
  pages of music, but also with traditions—
  kissing the *mezuzah*,
  lighting candles in times of trouble and
  times of prayer,
  sewing linens for brides-to-be . . .

And every Friday, before Shabbat, *Nona* gave Flory and her cousins baskets filled with food to take to neighbors in need.
Ts'daka!
"Don't wait for them to say 'thank you,'" *Nona* said.
"*We* are fortunate that we can give to them."

"ts'daka" charity

In *Nona*'s house, the little key—
la yave de Espanya—
watched over the family.
Nona told Flory its story:

"Many centuries ago, our ancestors
had no choice but to leave the
country they loved. They could not
take much with them. But they did
take the key to their home. That
key on the wall opens the door to a
beautiful house in Spain. One day
an Altaras will return to Spain,
find the house, open the door—and
be home once again!"

Flory loved the story, but she
didn't want to be the Altaras
who returned to Spain . . .
because she never wanted to
leave Vlasenica.

But her parents wanted to leave.
They liked the big city.
Goodbye, village.
Zagreb, in Croatia, had
    a brand new beautiful school,
    music lessons, art, ballet, gymnastics, theater.
But it did not have *Nona*, *Nonu*, *tiyas*,
    uncles, cousins, friends,
Shabbat baskets.
It did not have the songs.
Flory missed Vlasenica.
Her father saw her sorrow,
    and bought her a *harmoniku*.
Flory played the songs of her *Nona*,
    and they helped her feel closer to home.

"*harmoniku*"
accordion

1934

A terrible war came—the Second World War.

Life became dangerous, especially for Jews.

Flory's parents wanted her to be safe, and to be safe she needed to leave Zagreb.

They got her a train ticket to another city, called Split.

They would follow, they promised, on another train, another day.

It was too risky for three Jews to travel together.

"Florica," her father said, "from the minute you sit in that train compartment, don't speak!" He feared Flory might say something in Ladino, revealing that she was Jewish. "Just play your *harmoniku*." Flory took off the badge that all Jews had to wear and walked to the station, pretending to be an ordinary girl— a non-Jewish girl— going on a trip.

1941

She played and played
every song she knew—
Bosnian, Croatian, but not
a word in Ladino.
The compartment filled with
people, all joining together to
sing, all believing Flory was
one of them.
Such a jolly journey!
—for everyone else.
Flory hugged her *harmoniku* close,
and it saved her.

Flory reached the seaside city of Split, and her parents soon joined her.
They lived as refugees, without a home,
   not knowing what would happen to them,
   not knowing what happened to those left behind in Vlasenica.
And when the fighting finally ended . . .

Flory and her parents learned that the war had taken nearly everyone they loved.

Like her ancestors who fled Spain, Flory sailed away.
Unlike her ancestors, Flory carried no little key—
    not from Spain, not from Vlasenica.
Those keys were lost in the war.

But Flory carried three other
    precious possessions:
one, her *harmoniku*;
two, Ladino;
and three, bigger than everything,
yet taking up no space at all:

MUSIC.

1946

She was Flory Jagoda now, an American
with an American husband and family.
Her American family could never meet
her *Nona* or hear The Singing Altaras Family.
But . . . Flory could share their music.

She did have a key, after all—
    and with this key of music she unlocked the door
    to that past life and those beloved people,
    across the ocean and across the years.

Flory brought her music to people everywhere,
    around the country and the world,
    on stages, in schools, in homes.
Playing guitar—as her *Nona* played guitar—
    she could take audiences through the streets of her village,
    show them the roses in the windows,
    seat them at her *tiyas*' Passover tables . . .
    and even imagine a house in Spain,
    waiting, forever waiting, for an Altaras to return.

More About Flory Jagoda and Her Music

Flory was born in Bosnia on December 21, 1923. For much of her childhood, she lived in her grandparents' house in Vlasenica (VLA-seh-NITZ-uh). By the time World War II ended, Flory was a young woman. She went to work in Italy, where she and an American soldier, Harry Jagoda, fell in love and married. Before moving to the United States, Flory received the horrifying news that forty-two members of the Altaras (AL-ta-retz) family in her village had been killed in the Holocaust.

In the U.S., Flory dedicated herself to raising her four children—and to performing, teaching, and writing Sephardic songs in Ladino. She became known worldwide as the "Keeper of the Flame" of Sephardic music. In 2002, Flory was honored as a National Endowment for the Arts Heritage Fellow, an award recognizing the most significant folk artists in the United States.

Ladino, also called Judeo-Spanish, has existed for centuries. Today, few people know or speak the language. But if you have ever celebrated Hanukkah, chances are good that you have heard Ladino and already know Flory's music! Her famous song "Ocho Kandelikas" ("Eight Little Candles") is sung, in Ladino, at Hanukkah celebrations around the world.

A last note, about the very first sentence in this book: "Long ago, in a place called Al-Andalus in the land of Spain, there was . . . harmony among neighbors—Muslims, Jews, and Christians." Under this period of Muslim rule in Spain (from 711 to 1492), Jews did not have full citizenship rights. But despite these restrictions, the Altaras family carried with them memories of a good life before the Christian conquest of Spain in 1492.

"Oh, it is not me who is singing. It is my Nona."

—Flory Jagoda

Scan the QR code and watch Flory Jagoda sing her Ladino Hanukkah song "Ocho Kandelikas"